# Verity Fairy and Rapunzel

Written by Caroline Wakeman
Illustrated by Amy Zhing

# Contents

Fairy Tale Kingdom
Rapunzel's Tower
Cinderella's House
Enchanted Tree
Fairy Godmother's House
Prince Charming's Castle
Seven Dwarfs' House

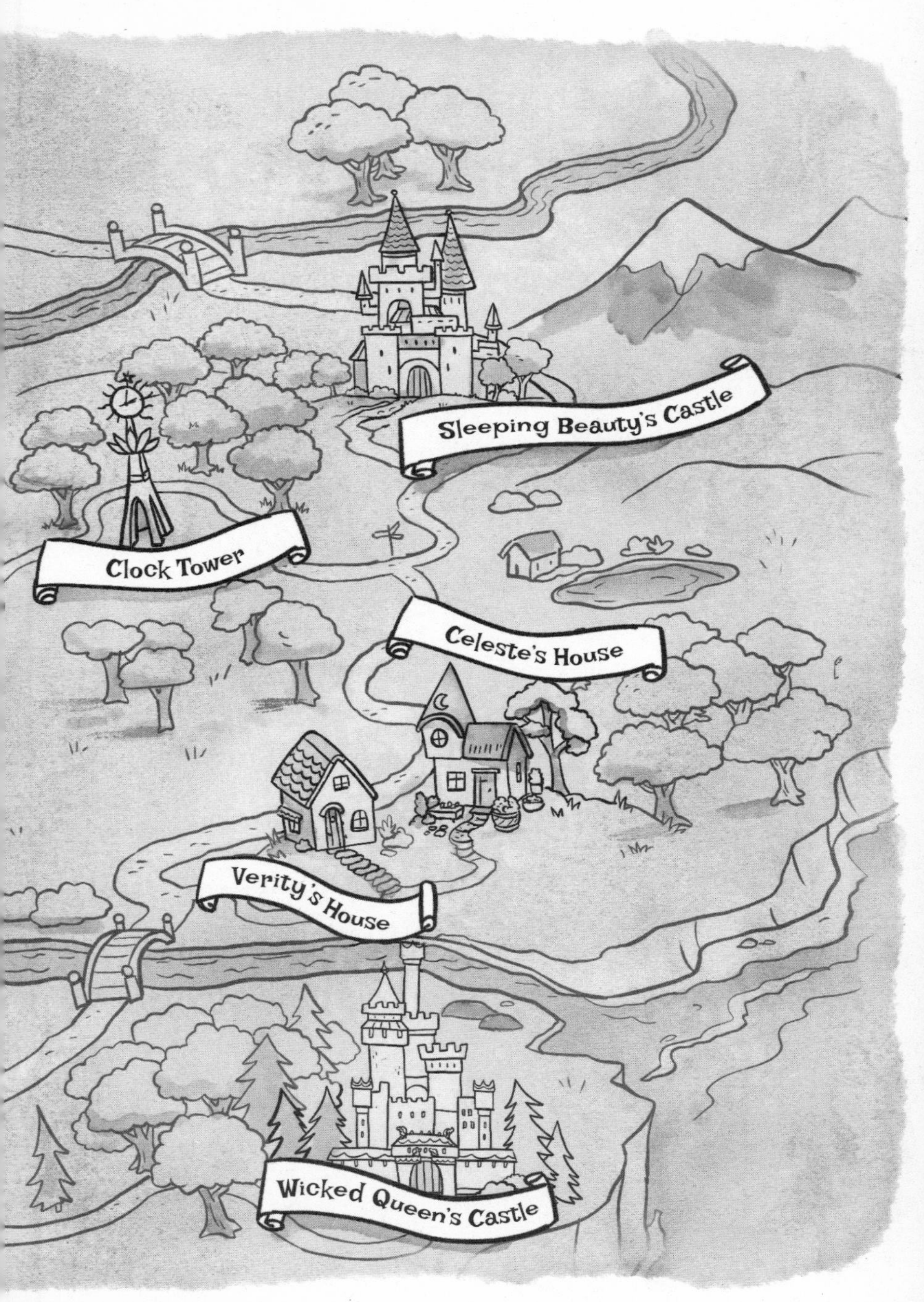
Sleeping Beauty's Castle
Clock Tower
Celeste's House
Verity's House
Wicked Queen's Castle

## Chapter One

# Verity's Important Job

Frost twinkled on the dark ground around the enchanted tree. High above, a bright full moon glowed. All the fairies huddled together to keep warm. Their job was to keep everyone happy and safe in the Fairy Tale Kingdom. Each month, Tatiana, the Queen of the Fairies, held a ceremony.

The fairy who had worked the hardest was rewarded with a special star.

Verity and Celeste stood next to each other. Their eyes sparkled with excitement. They were the best of friends and loved spending time together. They liked having flying races and reading their favorite magazine, *Sparkle Time*.

Verity crossed her fingers. "Who do you think the winner will be?" she asked.

Celeste reached up to check her hair. "Probably Fleur or Dawn. They both had the most important jobs this month."

Verity nervously played with her rainbow-colored skirt. She really wanted to be the first fairy to win a rare lilac star.

Everyone stopped talking as Tatiana stood in front of them. "And the winner is—Fleur!"

All the fairies clapped and cheered. Fleur stepped forward and opened a large magical box.

Verity gasped loudly. "Oh, pickled pumpkins!" she cried. "It's lilac!"

"No, it's not," whispered Celeste. "Watch."

A light blue star floated out of the box and drifted up into the sky before landing in Fleur's hands.

"Phew!" Verity said, relieved. She was very happy for Fleur, but secretly Verity felt that Tatiana didn't give her as many jobs as the other fairies. Verity thought she knew why. She had a habit of telling the truth—ALL the time—and that often caused her problems.

"Are you okay?" Celeste put her arm around Verity.

Verity shrugged. "I don't think I'll ever win a lilac star," she said glumly.

Celeste could see Tatiana waiting behind Verity to talk to her. "I think now might be your chance," she whispered.

Verity turned around and smiled broadly.

"Verity, I have a very important job for you." Tatiana's kind eyes grew serious. "I would like you to keep Rapunzel company in the tower. The Wicked Witch locked her away and Rapunzel is very lonely. The tower has just one small window, very high up, so it's impossible for Rapunzel to get out."

Verity shook her head. "Poor Rapunzel. Wait a minute! How does the Wicked Witch get in and out? Perhaps Rapunzel could do the same?"

"I don't think so. The Wicked Witch uses Rapunzel's **extremely** long hair to climb up and down the tower."

Verity tried climbing her own hair, but she kept falling down.

Tatiana smiled. "I think you'll cheer Rapunzel up."

"I like making new friends," Verity said happily. "I'll take my magazine. It's full of lots of fun things for us to talk about!"

**extremely** Very

SPARKLE
TIME

## Chapter Two
# Verity's New Friend

The next morning, Verity flew over a babbling stream and through the **dense** forest to a clearing where a tall gray-bricked tower with a bright red roof stood. As she approached the small window at the top of the tower, she could hear Rapunzel singing. Verity quickly placed her hands over her ears.

---

**dense** Containing lots of things closely packed together

"Eek! Someone needs singing lessons!" she said to herself with a little giggle.

A tall girl was brushing her extremely long hair.

"Wow—your hair is super long!" exclaimed Verity.

"Um, thank you..." Rapunzel was surprised to see Verity.

"I'm Verity. Tatiana, the Queen of the Fairies, sent me to keep you company... I'm a fairy, by the way." Verity showed Rapunzel her wand as proof. "You can't dip it in honey and stick it behind your ear. I did that once and my friend Celeste had to cut it out of my hair!"

Rapunzel smiled. "I'm not allowed to cut my hair, but I do love honey!"

"Me too!" nodded Verity. "Do you like blueberries?"

"They're delicious! Do you like strawberries?" Rapunzel asked eagerly.

"Absolutely! This is going to be such fun! Do you read *Sparkle Time?*" Verity pulled out the latest copy of the magazine from her backpack.

Rapunzel looked at it in amazement. "Wow! Look at all these different-colored wands you can buy!"

"It also has Snow White's tips for healthy eating." Verity pointed to Snow White on the front cover. "And there's a free bottle of Sprinkle-it-Better potion. I should carry that around with me. It would be useful if anyone hurts themselves. One of the seven dwarfs is always walking into things," she chuckled.

Verity and Rapunzel spent hours looking through *Sparkle Time* together. As they reached the end, Verity could see Rapunzel looked glum. "Have I upset you?" she asked. Verity twiddled her pink hair nervously.

Rapunzel shook her head sadly and a tear rolled down her cheek. "It's just that I've never seen so many interesting and colorful things before. I'd love to smell the flowers, lie in the grass, and go to parties and meet new people. Just like you!"

"Like me?" Verity was shocked.

"You're so lucky, Verity. You have your own house, a best friend who would do anything for you, and you're friends with Prince Charming!"

Verity could feel her cheeks redden. She had **exaggerated** how well she knew Prince Charming!

Verity and Rapunzel smiled weakly at each other. Verity wasn't sure what to say next. She didn't want to make Rapunzel sad again.

---

**exaggerated** Made it more than it really is

There was a long silence. Then Rapunzel said quietly, "I'd just like to read my book now."

While Rapunzel read, Verity sneaked out of the tower. She flew down to the stream below to think. She needed to come up with something different to talk about—something that didn't involve making Rapunzel feel like she was missing out.

## Chapter Three
# Rapunzel's Prince

As Verity sat looking at her sad **reflection** in the stream, another reflection appeared next to hers.

"What's wrong?" Celeste asked Verity gently.

"I don't know what to talk to Rapunzel about!" Verity admitted.

Celeste laughed. "You don't know what

---

**reflection** Image seen in a mirror or water

to talk about? That's not possible. I've never known you to run out of things to say before!"

"Every time I talk about something, it just reminds Rapunzel that she has never been anywhere but in the tower!" Verity tried to wipe her eyes without Celeste seeing.

"Verity, are you crying?" She handed Verity a tissue.

"I really like Rapunzel. She told me how much she wants to explore and meet new people."

Celeste jumped as Verity blew her nose loudly. It sounded like an elephant trumpeting.

"She had never even heard of Prince Charming!" Verity said dramatically.

"Wow! I thought everyone in the Fairy Tale Kingdom knew who Prince Charming was!" Celeste was shocked.

Verity shoved the used tissue back into Celeste's pocket.

"Instead of talking, why don't you do something together?" suggested Celeste. "Like dancing or sewing or—"

"I know!" Verity interrupted gleefully. "I could give her singing lessons—she's terrible!"

"O...kay!" Celeste had heard Verity's singing before and, although she wouldn't tell her, she didn't think her voice was very good either! However, Celeste was pleased Verity seemed happier. "Just call me if you need anything else," she said.

*

When Rapunzel had finsihed reading, Verity spent a long time teaching her to sing. But no matter how hard Rapunzel tried, she just didn't sound the same as Verity.

Suddenly, they heard a voice calling from the ground below.

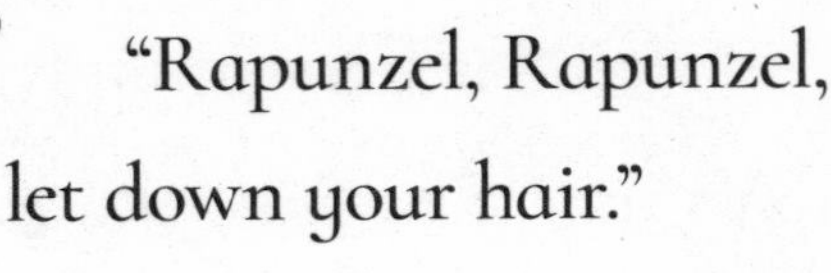

"Rapunzel, Rapunzel, let down your hair."

At once, Rapunzel ran over to the small window and let her braid fall down to the ground below. Verity could see a tall boy with kind eyes and a dazzling smile, calling up to the window.

"Who's that?" Verity asked Rapunzel.

"My prince."

"A real prince?" Verity was shocked that Rapunzel hadn't mentioned him before.

"He heard me singing one day and called up to me," Rapunzel said eagerly.

Verity nodded her head knowingly. "Oh, I see. So, he gives you singing lessons?"

"Actually, he said that I had a beautiful singing voice," said Rapunzel blushing. "We sit and talk and read books together. But he doesn't come to see me very often. The Wicked Witch has forbidden me from having visitors."

The prince was very **agile**. Verity and Rapunzel hardly had to help him up. Within a few seconds he had climbed through the window and into the tower. The prince removed his crown, sat down opposite Rapunzel and they talked for ages.

Verity could see how happy Rapunzel was. She was determined to find a way for

---

**agile** Move quickly and easily

Rapunzel to spend more time with the prince.

*

After the prince had left, Verity heard another voice calling up to the window.

"Rapunzel, Rapunzel, let down your hair!" cackled the Wicked Witch.

Rapunzel let her braid **cascade** down to the ground. Verity peered out of the window. Below was an old lady dressed in black, with a pointy nose and small beady eyes.

Verity screwed up her face. "She sounds very scary!" she said.

Verity and Rapunzel heaved the Wicked Witch up the tower. It seemed to take ages. "She needs to practice at Rock and Wall," said Verity.

"What's Rock and Wall?" Rapunzel asked.

---

 **cascade** Fall down

"Oh, it's great! They have these huge walls that you can practice climbing up with a rope. Teachers show you how to do it safely. After a few lessons, I'll bet she would be even quicker than the prince!" Verity said loudly. So loudly, that the Wicked Witch heard her.

"A prince?" shouted the Wicked Witch. She clumsily climbed through the window and fell onto the floor with a clatter.

## Chapter Four
# Fairy Dust

"Who's this?" The Wicked Witch prodded a bony finger at Verity, which knocked the little fairy flying.

Rapunzel quickly stepped between them. "This is Verity. She's here to keep me company."

"Oh, she is?" replied the Wicked Witch sternly. "I don't like fairies! And I told you, no visitors!" she **snarled**.

---


**snarled** Said in an angry way

The Wicked Witch sat down on the chair across from Rapunzel and suddenly jumped back up. "Is this yours?" she asked Verity crossly as she picked up the prince's crown which he had accidentally left behind.

"I don't wear a crown! That obviously belongs to the prince!" **scoffed** Verity without thinking.

"Oh no!" gasped Rapunzel.

The Wicked Witch glared at Verity. "You annoying little fairy!" she shrieked. She raised her wand to cast an evil spell.

Verity was desperate to fly out of the way, but the Wicked Witch's cackling laugh was so loud and terrifying that Verity found it impossible to move. Her little wings just wouldn't work!

---

**scoffed** Said in a mean, teasing way

*

Meanwhile, Celeste was busy putting away all the ingredients she had used to make fairy cakes. She packed the cakes into her picnic basket. She even remembered some powdered sugar to sprinkle on top. Then she flew over to Rapunzel's tower.

As she arrived, she heard an ear-piercing cackle. Her heart began to race. She knew that Verity was in trouble—big trouble!

Inside, Celeste saw the Wicked Witch lifting her wand.

"I'm going to enjoy turning you into a pile of dust!" she hissed.

As quick as a flash, Celeste flew into the tower and pulled Verity out through the open window.

"Ha! It worked!" cried the Wicked Witch happily as Verity disappeared. The Wicked Witch excitedly hopped and skipped around the tower. Celeste quickly poured her powdered sugar onto the windowsill.

"Look!" shouted the Wicked Witch pointing to the powdered sugar. "That's what happens to annoying little fairies—one wave of my wand and they're dust!"

"But Verity was my friend!" Rapunzel cried.

"Stop **sniveling**. I'm your friend!" snapped the Wicked Witch. "You don't need anyone else. Now out of my way, I need to get back down." Slowly the Wicked Witch used Rapunzel's braid to lower herself to the ground.

Celeste and Verity waited until the Wicked Witch had gone. Then they flew back inside to be with Rapunzel.

"Don't cry." Verity put her arm around Rapunzel. "Celeste saved me from the Wicked Witch's evil spell!"

"Verity!" gasped Rapunzel. "I can't believe you're okay." She was so relieved to see her fairy friend.

---

 **sniveling** Crying softly

“I’m usually super-fast at flying,” explained Verity. “But the Wicked Witch made me so scared that my wings wouldn’t work!”

“She scares me, too,” agreed Rapunzel. They talked for ages about all the things they found scary. Celeste left the fairy cakes on the table for Verity and Rapunzel and flew home. She was very happy that Verity and Rapunzel were becoming good friends.

Back in the tower, Verity was having lots of fun with Rapunzel. "I know! We could pretend we're going to a party!" said Verity excitedly. "In *Sparkle Time*, there are some party masks that we can cut out."

"Oh yes, that would be such fun!" Rapunzel squealed with delight.

Verity knew she had to be careful using scissors. As she cut out the masks, she told Rapunzel about the party where Cinderella met her prince. But as she dramatically described the clock striking midnight, she swung her scissors around and accidentally cut off Rapunzel's braid!

"Uh-oh!" Verity cried in shock.

"Is that what Cinderella said when the clock struck twelve?" asked Rapunzel.

"No," squeaked Verity. "That's what I say when I've done something silly!"

"What do you mean?" Rapunzel said slowly.

"I'm really sorry, Rapunzel," cried Verity. "I accidentally... cut... your... hair!"

Rapunzel grabbed the end of the bed to steady herself, her face going as white as the sheets. "The Wicked Witch will be very angry," she murmured.

Suddenly, a dreadful sound came from the ground below.

"Rapunzel, Rapunzel, let down your hair," demanded the Wicked Witch.

"What should we do?" cried Rapunzel.

"Okay—DON'T PANIC!" Verity took several deep breaths.

"I'm not panicking," replied Rapunzel calmly.

"Not you—me!" Verity flew rapidly around the room. "Think!"

"I'm thinking," Rapunzel sat down and placed her **index finger** on her cheek.

"Not you—me!" Verity said as she hovered anxiously in front of Rapunzel. "Oh, pickled pumpkins!" cried Verity. "The Wicked Witch will definitely turn me into fairy dust now!"

---

 **index finger** Finger next to the thumb

## Chapter Five

# Rapunzel's Braid

Verity needed to find a way to help Rapunzel and fast! As she stared at Rapunzel's long braid, an idea popped into her head. They still had exactly what they needed to pull the Wicked Witch up the tower.

"We can still use your hair," Verity cried excitedly. Rapunzel stared blankly back at Verity. "We'll tie one end of your braid to your bedpost and throw the other end out of the window. Then the Wicked Witch can climb up. Once she's in the tower, I will fly behind your head and hold the braid. The Wicked Witch will never know that we've cut your hair and then she won't be angry!"

"Verity, you're a genius!"

Verity smiled weakly. She didn't know what that meant.

They tied one end of the braid to the bedpost and threw the other end down to the Wicked Witch. Slowly they pulled her to the top.

The Wicked Witch tumbled through the window and fell onto the floor. As she stood up, Verity quickly untied the braid from the bedpost. She flew behind Rapunzel and held the braid against her head, keeping very still so that the Wicked Witch couldn't see her.

"That was hard work," said the Wicked Witch breathlessly. "Hmm, let me look at your braid." She pulled it closer, but Verity wasn't ready and the braid slipped through her fingers.

The Wicked Witch grabbed the end of

the braid and stared at it in horror. “I told you never to cut your hair!” she shouted.

Then from the ground below came a **familiar** voice.

**familiar** Well-known

"Rapunzel, Rapunzel, let down your hair!" cried the prince.

The Wicked Witch glared at Rapunzel. "So there is a prince that visits you! Well, not for much longer!"

The Wicked Witch threw one end of Rapunzel's long braid down to the prince.

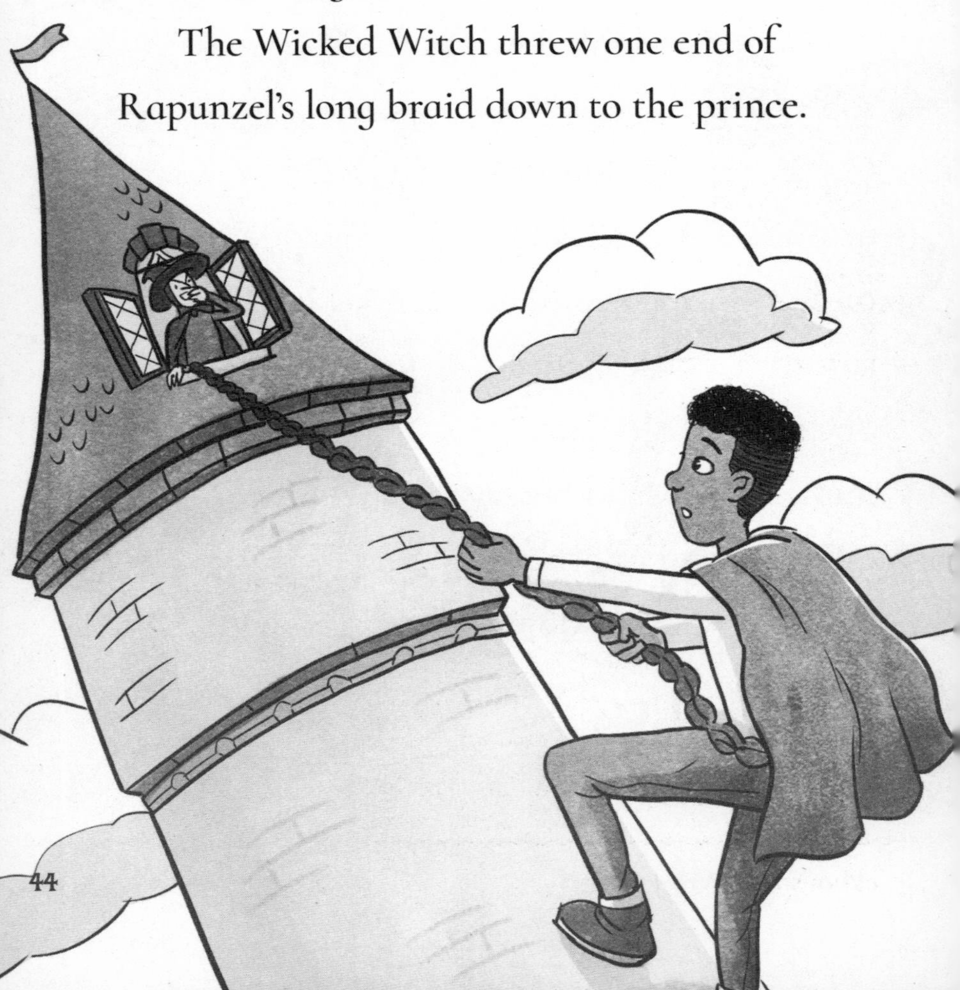

He climbed straight into her trap. As he reached the window, the Wicked Witch gave an evil laugh. Startled, the prince lost his balance. Toppling backward, he landed on a prickly bush far below.

Rapunzel sank down to the floor and sobbed.

"What should I do with YOU?" grumbled the Wicked Witch. She paced up and down the room, trying to think of a suitable punishment for Rapunzel.
She spotted the fairy cakes Celeste had made and helped herself to one. And another, and another, until she'd finished them all! She sat down, **exhausted** from trying to think of an evil plan, and quickly fell fast asleep.

---

**exhausted** Very tired

Rapunzel looked down at the poor prince lying dazed on the ground. He tried to sit up, but he was very wobbly. He couldn't see anything but stars.

"Don't worry," said Verity quietly. "We'll think of a way to help him before the Wicked Witch wakes up." She gave her friend a comforting hug. But in fact, Verity had completely run out of ideas.

## Chapter Six

# Sprinkle-it-Better

Verity was so busy trying to think of how to save the prince that she didn't see Celeste appear at the window.

"Oh no! What happened?" Celeste asked anxiously.

"The Wicked Witch did it!" Verity shook her head sadly. "If only there was a way to make him better."

"Sprinkle-it-Better!" said Celeste.

"Yes, but with what?" Verity was confused.

Celeste giggled. "It's the name of the free potion in this week's *Sparkle Time*. I saw it on the front of your magazine. It will help the prince see again!" Celeste said happily.

"Pickled pumpkins!" Verity checked to see if the Wicked Witch was still asleep and flew down to the prince. She sprinkled some of the potion over him and within seconds he was jumping to his feet.

"Rapunzel, Rapunzel, let down your hair," called the prince.

"I have another idea," Verity said proudly as she flew back inside the tower. "Let's tie one end of the braid around Rapunzel's bedpost again. Then we'll throw the other end out of the window. That way, Rapunzel can climb down her own hair to the ground."

"Ooh, I LOVE that idea!" Rapunzel had already started climbing out of the window.

"Thank you, Verity," she said joyfully. "You have saved me. I can't wait to travel around the Fairy Tale Kingdom with the prince and meet new people. You'll always be my best fairy friend."

Verity swallowed hard. She silently waved goodbye as Rapunzel and the prince rode away on his horse. Verity was very happy for them both, but she was going to miss Rapunzel.

Celeste put her arm around Verity. "Don't worry," said Celeste. "You and I can still have lots of fun together."

Verity smiled. "Thank goodness I've got you!"

The two fairies quickly flew out of the tower before the Wicked Witch had a chance to wake up. They left Rapunzel's braid tied to the bedpost so she could climb down to the ground.

## Chapter Seven

# Rapunzel's Gift

A few days later, Celeste flew past the tower and heard a familiar voice from inside.

"So, here's your membership to Rock and Wall," Verity explained. She handed the Wicked Witch her card. "They have races each week to see who can reach the top of the wall first."

"And is the prize a prince? I'd really like to have my own prince to keep!" cackled the Wicked Witch.

"No!" Verity frowned. "Why do you want to keep your own prince?"

"So I can talk to him. Being a witch is very lonely, you know. That's why I locked Rapunzel away in the tower. It meant I always had someone to talk to," the Wicked Witch said sadly.

“Oh, now I understand,” said Verity. She had never thought that the Wicked Witch might be lonely. “Well, each month at Rock and Wall, they have a special event called ‘Witch Wall’ where you can meet lots of other witches! It sounds like fun!”

"Ooh!" The Wicked Witch sounded interested. "Do you think I'll make some new friends?"

"Oh yes," Verity said confidently. "And then you'll never need to lock anyone in a tower ever again!"

*

The next night, the full moon shone brightly in the starry sky. Tatiana had gathered all the fairies around the enchanted tree. She was going to present one lucky fairy with a special sparkly star.

"I think it will be you!" Celeste said to Verity excitedly.

Verity held her breath.

"This star goes to the fairy who completed a difficult task," Tatiana announced.

"But she also went out of her way to be kind. Verity, you kept Rapunzel company and helped the Wicked Witch make friends. Now she is no longer lonely. Good job—we're all very proud of you!"

All the fairies clapped and cheered.

Verity beamed as a beautiful turquoise sparkly star floated up into the sky above.

Slowly it drifted down and landed in Verity's hands.

"Thank you very much," said Verity happily to Tatiana. Although it wasn't the lilac star that Verity dreamed of winning, she still loved it!

Tatiana then handed Verity a box and a postcard.

"Ooh, what's that?" Celeste picked up the postcard and read it aloud.

*"To my best fairy friend, Verity.*
*I'm having a wonderful time exploring the Fairy Tale Kingdom. I love meeting new people and I have been to lots of parties. I am sending you a little gift as a reminder of our time together.*
*I hope you like it!*
*Your friend, Rapunzel."*

Verity opened up the box and pulled out a beautiful white and sparkly party mask with feathers at the top.

"Do you like it?" Celeste asked eagerly. She really wanted Verity to be happy with the mask.

"It's wonderful!" Verity whispered. "All I need now is an invitation to Prince Charming's next party."

"But he won't recognize you behind a mask," said Celeste.

"He will if I sing to him. Everyone knows my amazing singing voice!" Verity said proudly.

Celeste giggled. "You're one of a kind, Verity!"

# Fairy Quiz

1

What is the name of Verity and Celeste's favorite magazine?

2

How does the witch climb up the tower to Rapunzel?

3

What did Celeste pour onto the windowsill to make the witch think she had turned Verity into dust?

4

What did Verity accidentally cut off?

5
What is the name of the potion that Verity used to help the prince?
6
What is the name of the place that Verity gave the Wicked Witch a membership to?
7
What color is the star that Tatiana gave to Verity?
8
What gift did Rapunzel give Verity at the end?

## Answers

1. *Sparkle Time* 2. She uses Rapunzel's long hair 3. Powdered sugar 4. Rapunzel's braid 5. Sprinkle-it-Better 6. Rock and Wall 7. Turquoise 8. A party mask

**Written by** Caroline Wakeman
**Illustrated by** Amy Zhing
**Designed by** Collaborate Agency
**Fiction Editor** Heather Featherstone
**Educational Consultants** Jacqueline Harris, Jenny Lane-Smith
**Senior Editors** Amy Braddon, Marie Greenwood
**US Senior Editor** Shannon Beatty
**Senior Designer** Ann Cannings
**Managing Editor** Laura Gilbert
**Managing Art Editor** Diane Peyton Jones
**Production Editor** Rob Dunn
**Production Controller** Francesca Sturiale
**Publishing Manager** Francesca Young
verityfairy.com

First American Edition, 2021
Published in the United States by DK Publishing

1450 Broadway, Suite 801, New York, New York 10018


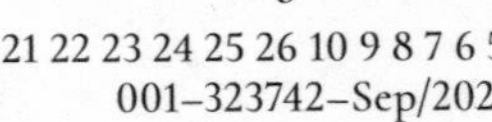

21 22 23 24 25 26 10 9 8 7 6 5 4 3 2 1
001–323742–Sep/2021

Published in Great Britain by Dorling Kindersley Limited.

A catalog record for this book is available from the Library of Congress.
ISBN: 978-0-7440-3935-1 (Paperback)
ISBN: 978-0-7440-3936-8 (Hardcover)

Printed and bound in Great Britain by
Clays Ltd, Elcograf S.p.A.

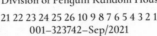

For the curious
**www.dk.com**

This book was made with Forest Stewardship Council™ certified paper – one small step in DK's commitment to a sustainable future. For more information go to www.dk.com/our-green-pledge